PUFFIN BOOKS

Mattie and Grandpa

Mattie's family have come to pay their last respects to Grandpa who is lying in bed, close to death. Most of them are crying ... but not Mattie. He's too busy watching a fly on the ceiling chasing something very small. He is wondering if that something very small might fall off and tickle Grandpa because Grandpa is much too ill to scratch himself. Then, surprisingly, Grandpa speaks to Mattie. He asks Mattie to go for a walk. Together they set off on an incredible journey into the land of make-believe. A magical land of rivers, mountains, sunflowers, horses and a few pirates. But one thing is troubling Mattie. The further they travel, the smaller Grandpa gets until he is just a little speck on Mattie's hand.

A simple, poignant story showing that special relationship that often exists between the very young and the very old. A story of family love which lasts for ever.

Roberto Piumini is one of Italy's foremost children's authors. Born in Brescia, Italy, his previous jobs include teaching, acting and working with children's drama groups. He has published several highly regarded contemporary fiction and poetry titles for children and teenagers in Italy. A modern writer and story-teller of exceptional talent, his fame is now spreading into Europe.

ROBERTO PIUMINI

Mattie and Grandpa

Illustrated by Anthony Lewis
Translated from the Italian by
Isabel Quigly

PUFFIN BOOKS

PUFFIN BOOKS

Published by the Penguin Group
Penguin Books Ltd, 27 Wrights Lane, London W8 5TZ, England
Penguin Books USA Inc., 375 Hudson Street, New York, New York 10014, USA
Penguin Books Australia Ltd, Ringwood, Victoria, Australia
Penguin Books Canada Ltd, 10 Alcorn Avenue, Toronto, Ontario, Canada M4V 3B2
Penguin Books (NZ) Ltd, 182–190 Wairau Road, Auckland 10, New Zealand

Penguin Books Ltd, Registered Offices: Harmondsworth, Middlesex, England

First published by Einaudi Ragazzi
Copyright © Edizioni E. Elle, Trieste, Italy 1993
Published in Puffin Books 1993
1 3 5 7 9 10 8 6 4 2

Text copyright © Roberto Piumini, 1993
English translation copyright © Isabel Quigly, 1993
Illustrations copyright © Anthony Lewis, 1993
All rights reserved

The moral right of the author has been asserted

Typeset by DatIX International Limited, Bungay, Suffolk
Filmset in Monophoto Palatino
Printed in England by Clays Ltd, St Ives plc

1

Grandpa was lying in bed, very pale, thin and slight. Around him were Mum, Dad, two uncles, six grandchildren and several family friends. They were all in tears, or on the point of crying, or had just been crying – except for the youngest grandchild, who was eight and called Mattie.

Some of them were looking at Grandpa, who had his eyes shut and was breathing slowly, his chest rising and falling very slightly. Some of them were looking at his thin, still hands which were hardly less white than the sheets. Some were looking at the side of the bed, where there was a red fringe. Some had their eyes shut and were looking at the darkness inside them.

Mattie was looking at a fly walking on the ceiling, just above Grandpa, which didn't seem to know where to go. It would move in one direction, then in another, forwards a bit, backwards a bit: maybe it had lost something very small, and was looking for it.

Mattie thought that something which is small to a fly must be tiny to a little boy, and even more tiny to a grown-up. He thought that the tiny thing the fly was looking for might have fallen off the ceiling, because things did fall down, except for flies, which were stuck on with hooks:

Grandpa had once told him so. And Mattie thought that the tiny thing which had fallen off the ceiling must have landed right on Grandpa, who was lying there. And maybe that tiny thing was now tickling Grandpa. And he thought that if he knew where Grandpa was feeling ticklish he could scratch him, because it looked as if Grandpa wasn't able to scratch himself.

2

While he was thinking this, Grandpa turned
his head towards him and said:

'Mattie.'

The others never moved, perhaps because
Grandpa hadn't spoken to them. It seemed
as if they hadn't realized Grandpa had
spoken.

'Yes, Grandpa?' said Mattie, who was
looking up at the ceiling to watch the fly,
but lowered his head to answer. He thought
Grandpa was going to say where he wanted
to be scratched. Instead he said:

'Shall we go for a walk?'

Mattie looked around him. Maybe
because Grandpa had asked only him, the
others — Mum, Dad, his sisters, his uncles
and cousins — didn't move or speak, and
went on looking at Grandpa, or at his hands,
or at the counterpane, or at the darkness
through their tears.

This was a bit odd, but not impossible, considering what was happening.

'But aren't you dying, Grandpa?' said Mattie.

'Who says so?' said Grandpa, raising his hand and scratching the end of his nose.

'Everyone,' said Mattie, and turned his head to indicate the others there.

'They're teasing,' said Grandpa.

'Really?'

Mattie looked round at his family again, all silent and still, their expressions unchanged.

'They look very serious, Grandpa,' he said, and wanted to laugh.

'Well, yes,' said Grandpa. 'That's because they don't know about teasing.'

He raised himself and sat up in bed.

'Well, shall we go?'

'Where, Grandpa?'

'For a walk. Let's go for a nice one, the sort we like.'

'What shall I tell Mum?'

Mattie looked at her: her eyes were shut and her throat was trembling.

'If we're quiet, no one will notice,' said Grandpa, stretching his legs out on to the carpet.

In fact, no one did notice.

'Shall we be out long?' asked Mattie, glancing at Dad, who was looking at the counterpane's fringe.

'I don't know,' said Grandpa. 'With the best walks, you never can tell how long they'll last. But take your pullover, it may be windy.'

He got up, and took Mattie's hand.

Grandpa's hand was thin, warm and dry. Apart from Mum's face, it was the nicest thing to touch.

'Let's go,' said Mattie, as if the idea of going for a walk had been his.

They went to the door, while everyone was still looking at the bed. An uncle blew his nose, making a funny noise. One of Mattie's sisters gave a big sigh.

Mattie glanced at the ceiling behind him, to see if the fly was still searching. But it wasn't there any more.

Grandpa opened the door softly, as if he was trying not to wake someone.

3

Outside, there was no passage, or staircase, or front door, or street, or town.

On the left was a big field, and on the right a peaceful river, and you could hear the sound of running water.

Mattie and Grandpa were on the left bank of the river.

'This is the left bank, isn't it, Grandpa?' said Mattie.

'D'you think so?' said Grandpa, pressing his hand a little, but without turning. 'How d'you know?'

'Dad told me.'

'And how do we know we're on the left bank?'

Mattie took a deep breath.

'You've got to stand with your back to the mountain,' he said.

Grandpa turned back.

'But we haven't got a mountain behind

us,' he said.

'It's just a way of saying it,' said Mattie. 'It means we've got to have our backs to the place the water's coming from, d'you see? Like us now.'

'I see,' said Grandpa. 'It means that the river, there behind us, starts in the mountains, like all rivers.'

'That's right,' said Mattie, nodding vigorously to agree with Grandpa. 'Rivers never start at the sea.'

'Right. And so?' said Grandpa.

'When you've got your back to the mountain, the way we have now – which doesn't mean there's really a mountain – it's easy,' said Mattie. 'The bank on our left is the left bank, and the one on our right's the right bank. D'you follow me?'

'Yes, it's easy,' said Grandpa.

'We're on the left bank, and the one over there is the right bank,' said Mattie, just to be sure that his explanation was quite clear. 'D'you see?'

'I do,' said Grandpa. 'So now we're going towards the sea, aren't we?'

Mattie considered this for a moment.

'Quite right,' he said.

There was a thoughtful silence.

'And does the river know?' Grandpa asked.

'Know what?'

'Does the river know this is its left bank?'

Mattie laughed.

'I wonder! Maybe it doesn't care. Let's try asking it.'

And Mattie asked the river if it knew this was its left bank, and the other was its right bank. But the river said nothing, and carried on making its quiet sound of running water.

4

Beyond the river, on the right bank, there was a horse.

'Look!' said Grandpa.

It was white and looked very large. It was eating grass on the bank and moving its tail slowly back and forth.

'D'you like him?' said Grandpa, putting his free hand up to his eyes to see better beyond the glittering water.

'Oh yes,' said Mattie. 'But the river's in the way.'

He was looking at the horse in an odd way, shutting one eye and peering between the end of his first finger and the end of his thumb, as if he had it, very small, in his hand. Then he let go of Grandpa's hand and made his hands into a telescope: and the horse looked bigger.

'Let's give him a name,' said Grandpa. 'Maybe we'll meet him sooner or later.'

So they played at finding a name for the horse. They thought of a lot of names, but none of them was right.

'Chalky?'

'Mmm . . . Speedy?'

'Mmm . . . Windblown?'

'Mmm . . . Pegasus?'

'What's Pegasus, Grandpa?'

Grandpa told Mattie the story of the winged horse Pegasus.

'That's a good story,' said Mattie at the

end of it. 'But I don't think it's the right name.'

They tried again, then fell silent and looked at the river. The horse had moved a short way from the bank, to the right, facing the mountain. Now and then, as if he could feel Mattie and Grandpa looking at him, he raised his head and looked at them, keeping quite still. His mane flapped against his neck. Then he went back to grazing.

'Brigand. D'you like that?' asked Mattie.

'Yes,' said Grandpa.

'Right then, Brigand.'

They carried on walking towards the sea, and now and then Mattie turned to look at the horse.

'But if he's already got a name of his own, how can he also be called Brigand?' he said after a while.

'It's people who give names,' said Grandpa. 'If we give him the name Brigand, then he's Brigand as well.'

'So we're a bit his owners, because we've

given him a name,' said Mattie. 'He's a bit ours, is that it?'

'That's it,' said Grandpa.

Mattie turned, delightedly, and cupped his hands round his mouth.

'You're Brigand!' he shouted to the horse. 'Brigand! Hi, Brigand! D'you hear? Brigand!'

On the other side of the river, the horse lifted his white head. His tail rose too, and stayed up for a few moments.

'Fine! That's right! Brigand!' yelled Mattie, running up and down the bank.

The horse put his head down to the grass again.

'He heard, didn't he?' said Mattie, turning to Grandpa, who was holding out his hand.

'I think so,' said Grandpa. 'Horses have good hearing.'

5

A canal about two metres wide flowed out of the river, and ran between green fields to the left. The path ran beside it, and Mattie and Grandpa walked along it. It wasn't very deep, and the water plants were bent over by the current, while fish swam calmly above them.

'I'll catch some!' said Mattie, turning to Grandpa. 'Shall I?'

'How will you catch them?'

'With my hands.'

'You've got to be good at it. Have a try.'

Mattie gave a happy jump and then lay flat on the bank. He stayed there quietly, looking down into the green water. Grandpa sat beside him, watching in silence.

Suddenly Mattie plunged his hand in, splashing water up to his hair, but he didn't catch the fish. After a while he tried again, but he didn't manage it.

Then he changed tactics, using both hands, keeping them quite still in the water, like water weeds. He waited for a fish to come close and tried to catch him, but the fish whisked away like a green shadow in the canal.

'I can't do it, Grandpa.'

'Try again.'

He tried again, but didn't catch one, and his hands were cold.

'Let's change the way we do it,' said Grandpa.

He took off his shoes and socks, put them side by side on the bank, and very quietly went into the water.

'You're all wet, Grandpa!'

'I'll get dry afterwards,' said Grandpa, and stood in the middle of the canal, with his legs apart and his back to the current.

'Coming?' he said to Mattie. 'The sun's hot, we'll soon dry off. Don't you want to catch some fish?'

Mattie quickly unlaced his shoes and pulled off his socks.

'Shall I take off my trousers, too?' he asked.

'No, we need them for fishing,' said Grandpa.

With a shiver, Mattie got into the cool running water.

'Come here, like me,' said Grandpa, moving a little to the right to make room for Mattie, who spread his legs like him.

'What now, Grandpa?'

'We're going to fish.'

'Standing still like this?'

'As still as we can. But we've got to keep our pockets open, like this.'

Grandpa pulled his trouser pockets open, and Mattie did the same. He felt the water caressing his legs and thighs and the base of his spine.

'The water's tickling me!' he said.

'Me too,' said Grandpa, and they laughed together.

Suddenly Mattie felt something wriggling in his left pocket.

'Grandpa, I've caught one!'

'Close your pocket, then!'

Mattie closed up his pocket, while something wriggled inside it, tickling him more than the water.

'I've got one too,' said Grandpa.

'He's huge!' said Mattie, patting the outside of the wriggling, swollen pocket.

'Mine's not bad either,' said Grandpa.

'Shall I take him out?' said Mattie.

'Yes, but gently. Hold the pocket with one hand, and put the other hand in very carefully, moving the material. Otherwise, he'll get away.'

Standing together in the canal, Mattie and Grandpa slowly put their hands in their pockets. Mattie felt something cold, smooth and heavy, which trembled. He was a bit scared, but carried on. Very carefully, he grasped the fish's body and took it out of his pocket: it wasn't as big as he'd thought, but was a wonderful colour.

'Look, Grandpa!'

'Keep it in the water, or it'll die,' said Grandpa, who was taking a smaller fish than Mattie's out of his pocket. Both of them held their fish underwater.

'Now what?' said Mattie.

'Don't you want to eat it?' said Grandpa.

'Eat it?'

'People usually fish so as to eat what they catch,' said Grandpa.

Mattie looked at the fish, who was no longer moving much, as if he was tired. Now and then his tail flicked between Mattie's fingers.

'But I'm not hungry for fish,' he said. 'I don't want to eat him.'

He looked at Grandpa and had a funny feeling, as if Grandpa was different. But he wasn't: he was still Grandpa.

'I don't want to eat mine, either,' said Grandpa. 'We couldn't even cook them, we haven't got the gear.'

'Then let's let them go,' said Mattie.

'Good idea,' said Grandpa, opening his

hands: a dark shape glided towards the moving weeds on the canal bed, and vanished.

Mattie let his fish go too. As soon as he opened his hands it streaked away. But half a metre away it stopped uncertainly, as if it couldn't believe it was free.

'Carry on, Free Fish,' said Mattie. 'Mine is called Free Fish, Grandpa.'

The fish glided swiftly away, following the current.

'Shall we go on fishing?' asked Grandpa.

'No, we've done enough,' answered Mattie.

They got out of the canal, dripping, then took off their trousers and laid them out in the sun.

'Did you enjoy fishing?' asked Grandpa.

'Yes, I did,' said Mattie.

He looked into the canal, to see if he could see Free Fish. But among all the fishes there he couldn't recognize him.

'You'd need enormous pockets to catch a whale,' he said thoughtfully. 'Like circus clowns have.'

Grandpa said nothing, holding a blade of grass between his lips, and looking at the canal.

Looking at Grandpa, Mattie had a funny feeling again: but he didn't know what it was.

6

Further on, they came to a fork in the road.
The left-hand fork went ahead, along the
canal. The right fork crossed over a small
bridge and carried on along the river, a little
further from the bank.

'Which way shall we go, Grandpa?' said
Mattie.

'I don't know,' said Grandpa. 'You decide.'

Mattie looked at both roads. He liked the
one that went ahead, but he liked the bridge
road too, which went beside the river.

'I like both roads, Grandpa. I can't decide,'
he said. 'Shall we toss for it?'

'Right,' said Grandpa, putting his hand in
his pocket and taking out a couple of coins.

'Which one shall we toss with?' he asked.

Mattie took the coins and looked at them.
Both were very fine. One had a ship on one
side and an ear of corn on the other. The
second coin had a wheel on one side and a

bearded head on the other.

'I don't know which one to choose, Grandpa,' said Mattie. 'Because I like them both.'

'But which one d'you like best?' asked Grandpa.

Mattie looked at the coins again, turning them over, and then chose the one with the ship on it.

'Now we've got to say which road we'll take if the ear of corn comes up, and which one if the ship does.'

'I can't decide, Grandpa,' said Mattie, twiddling the coin round in his fingers.

'Think it over. There must be a way of deciding.'

Mattie looked at the coin and thought.

'Let's do this,' he said. 'If the ship comes up, we'll go left, because that's the road beside the water. If the ear of corn comes up we'll go right, because that's the road through the fields.'

'Fine,' said Grandpa. 'Toss!'

But just as he was going to toss the coin, Mattie stopped.

'I don't have to toss the coin, Grandpa,' he said.

'Why not?'

'I've made up my own mind which road to take.'

'Which one?'

'The one over the bridge.'

'Right.'

'D'you want to know why, Grandpa?'

'D'you want to tell me?'

'Yes.'

'Why have you chosen the road over the bridge, then?'

'Because the canal road goes too far away from the river. But the bridge road, you see, goes along the river, even if it passes through the fields.'

'That's true. And you want to be near the river, do you?'

'Yes, Grandpa.'

'Fine.'

'D'you want to know why?'

'D'you want to tell me?'

'Yes.'

'Why, then?'

'Because Brigand's across the river.'

'But he's on the other side,' said Grandpa.

'Yes. But sooner or later there'll be a bridge, won't there?'

'Yes, I should think so,' said Grandpa. 'We've found a little one here, across the canal. Later we'll find a big one, across the river.'

They set off along the bridge road, and walked through the fields. Mattie was playing with the two coins, and as he looked at Grandpa he had that same funny feeling.

7

A couple of kilometres on, they came to a
town: houses and a bell tower appeared.
The road through the fields led straight to
it. On the right, the river was close to them
again, though not as close as before. But
there was no sign of the horse on the other
bank.

'Grandpa, there may be a bridge in the town,' said Mattie.

'Maybe,' said Grandpa.

Suddenly Mattie stopped. He realized what the funny feeling was: Grandpa looked smaller. Not a lot, but certainly smaller.

'What's up, Mattie?'

Mattie thought that, for fear of scaring Grandpa, he shouldn't say anything.

'Nothing, Grandpa. I've got a stone in my shoe.'

'When I was a boy and felt tired, I used to say I had a stone in my shoe as well.'

'But I'm not tired, Grandpa.'

'Then it's really a stone. You'll have to take it out,' said Grandpa, and went on walking towards the town.

Mattie watched him carefully from behind.

He saw that Grandpa really had become smaller. He remembered that before he'd just come up to the belt of Grandpa's trousers: now he came higher up.

Mattie was a little worried, but not very

much. He could see that Grandpa looked fine, and was walking quickly ahead. In fact, he wasn't sorry that Grandpa was a little smaller: it meant that when he talked to him, he wouldn't have to look up so far.

Grandpa's clothes had become smaller too, he noticed.

'Just as well,' Mattie thought. 'Otherwise they'd be flapping round him, and he'd notice.'

Grandpa turned.

'Have you taken out the stone?' he asked.

'No,' said Mattie.

'Why not?'

'I've been thinking. I'll take it out now, Grandpa.'

Grandpa went on walking, without looking back again. Although there wasn't a stone in his shoe, Mattie bent down, took off his shoe and turned it upside-down. He felt that by doing this, he made the lie less serious.

8

The town wasn't as small as it had looked from a distance. They walked right up to the bell tower.

Grandpa stopped and looked up.

'You'd get a great view from up there,' he said. 'We might see if there was a bridge across the river.'

'Shall we go up, Grandpa?' Mattie cried. He'd never been up a bell tower.

'Let's see,' said Grandpa.

They went closer to the tower, and the closer they went the higher it seemed, right up in the sky. By the door was a little table, and sitting at the table was a man in a peaked cap.

'Can we go up the bell tower?' Grandpa said.

'If you pay,' said the man.

Grandpa fumbled in his pockets.

'I haven't got any money,' he said. 'Have you, Mattie?'

Mattie thought he'd find the two coins, but when he looked he couldn't find them.

'I can't find the coins, Grandpa,' he said tearfully.

'People who tell fibs lose their money — it's obvious you told a fib,' said Grandpa, and laughed. Then he turned to the bell-tower keeper and said:

'Let's play a game. If I win, you'll let us into the tower without paying. If I lose, I'll

give you my tie, which is silk.'

The keeper looked at the tie, and touched the open collar of his shirt.

'Right,' he said.

They played 'Paper, scissors, stone'. Mattie watched, but couldn't follow it, because they were playing very fast, flinging their hands on the table, either open or clenched, and using strange short words that were half numbers and half shouts. Their left hands, lying on the table top, kept the score.

Mattie watched, open mouthed. He'd never seen Grandpa playing 'Paper, scissors, stone', and he seemed very good at it. He saw that now and then Grandpa looked up at the keeper's face, whereas the keeper kept staring down at his hands.

At last the game finished.

'You're very good,' the keeper told Grandpa. 'You've won.'

'Only just,' said Grandpa. 'We were close, and I was mean.'

'Right then, go on up,' said the keeper, and opened the door of the bell tower.

It was dark and cool inside, smelling musty, and of ancient stone.

Grandpa turned, and gave Mattie his hand. It was hard to see anything.

'Let's wait a moment,' said Grandpa. 'Then we'll be able to see.'

9

Very, very gradually, they made out a steep wooden staircase.

'You go first,' said Grandpa. 'I'll come behind.'

'You're afraid I'll fall,' said Mattie, pausing with his hand on the rail.

'Yes,' said Grandpa.

'Suppose you fall?'

'You've got a point,' said Grandpa. 'But what can we do? We can't go up together, it's too narrow.'

'Let's do this,' said Mattie. 'You go behind for a bit, and I'll go behind for a bit. Whichever one of us is behind must be very careful where he steps.'

So they went up like that, changing places on each landing. They went very slowly, and as they went up they looked through the arrow slits and saw the roofs of the town becoming lower and lower below them.

They were red in the face and panting
when they reached the top. But a cool
breeze made them feel better at once.

The view was splendid. Below the red
roofs of the houses there were narrow
streets, and beyond them they could see a
small square with the coloured awnings of a
market. Green and yellow countryside
surrounded the town. The river gleamed
like a strip of metal, and beyond it the

country opened out to the hills on the horizon.

'There's a horse down there!' cried Mattie. 'But he's black. He's not Brigand.'

'I can see,' said Grandpa. 'And there's a bridge, too, further on, to the left.'

Mattie leant out a little to look, and the wind ruffled his hair.

'Is there always wind up here?' he said.

'Often,' said Grandpa. 'Nearly always, I should think.'

It was nice looking around: Mattie could have gone on looking for ever.

'Shall we go to the market, then?' said Grandpa.

'But we haven't got any money!' said Mattie, looking down at the coloured awnings.

'Who cares?' said Grandpa. 'We'll go and have a look. And if we like something, we'll take it!'

Mattie followed him down the stairs, frowning. What did Grandpa mean? That he

was going to steal things from the market?
Mattie didn't want to steal.

Grandpa, ahead of him, seemed to have
grown a little smaller still.

'Grandpa,' said Mattie.

'What's up?'

'I didn't have a stone in my shoe before.'

'I knew that.'

'How did you know?'

'Because you weren't hobbling.'

'I see. Well, I did tell a lie. I didn't stay
behind because I had a stone in my shoe.'

'I told you a lie too,' said Grandpa.

'What?'

'When I told you that people who tell
fibs lose their money.'

'But I really did lose the money! Maybe I
lost it when I pretended to take out the
stone.'

'Maybe,' said Grandpa. 'Well, let's go
down now.'

They went on, down the wooden
staircase. Mattie could see that Grandpa was

smaller, and so were his clothes.

When they reached the bottom, they saw the keeper playing 'Paper, scissors, stone' on his own. He held his hand above the table, and then lowered it, open or clenched, or with several fingers stiff, and made that strange noise, half numbers and half shouts.

Grandpa stood watching him for a while.

'You're practising with your shadow, aren't you?' he said, after a bit.

'Yes,' said the keeper. 'When I'm quicker than my shadow, no one'll be able to beat me.'

'If I come back, we'll see!' said Grandpa, as he and Mattie set off for the square.

They could already hear the market noises in the distance.

10

The market opened out before Mattie and
Grandpa, beautiful and full of colours. There
were stalls of fabrics and sweets, fruit and
saucepans, tools and dresses, shoes, toys, all
kinds of things. Everyone was talking and
shouting, looking and buying.

'Is there anything you like?' Grandpa asked.

'But we haven't got any money!'

'Don't worry about that. Is there anything you like?'

Mattie wasn't sure. If Grandpa wanted to steal, it was best to make him steal something cheap. Among the cheap things near by, Mattie liked a corn cob.

'That,' he said.

'Are you hungry?' asked Grandpa.

'No. I like its colour and shape.'

'Right,' said Grandpa, and went over to the stall. He took off his tie and showed it to the seller.

'Can I buy a corn cob with this?' he asked.

The man pursed his lips and raised an eyebrow.

'Certainly,' he said. 'And a nice apple with it.'

He picked a big red apple and handed it to Mattie, and with his other hand gave Grandpa the corn cob. Then he took the tie, folded it carefully, and laid it beside the cash box.

'See, Mattie?' said Grandpa, and gave him the corn cob.

Mattie walked along behind Grandpa, with the apple in one hand and the corn cob in the other. He didn't know what to do. He had an apple and a corn cob, and he wasn't hungry. He had Grandpa, who was getting smaller and smaller. Mattie thought he now came up to his chest.

'Grandpa,' he said suddenly.

'Yes, Mattie?'

'I've got something I must tell you.'

'Must or want to?'

'Want to.'

'Tell me, then.'

Mattie was silent.

'Don't you want to?'

'Yes, I do.'

'Right, then.'

'You're getting smaller,' Mattie said with an effort.

'D'you mean I'm getting younger?'

'No, small in height. Small in size. You're becoming a little Grandpa.'

'Oh, that's good! That's why I feel so light,' said Grandpa.

'You don't mind?'

'No, I really don't.'

'Really not?'

Grandpa leant down towards Mattie, not the way he used to, because he was smaller now. He looked into Mattie's eyes.

'I don't mind, Mattie,' he said. 'I feel fine, and I'm all in one piece. Let's go on, now. Is there anything else you'd like?'

'No, thanks. I've already got the corn cob and the apple. But I'm not hungry, Grandpa. Are you?'

'No. Let's hang on to the corn cob and the apple, shall we? They may come in useful.'

They walked on through the market, listening to the voices, sniffing the smells, looking at the colours. Then they left the market and the town, and walked on towards the river and the bridge they had seen from the bell tower. But they couldn't find it.

As always, the sky was bright and cloudless.

11

They walked along the river without
speaking. Mattie was thinking of how
Grandpa was getting smaller, and now and
then had a look at him. Then he would look
back at the river. He could now see the
bridge, which was near by, and the
countryside on the opposite bank, and was
looking for the horse – but there was no
sign of him. Across the river there was a
big field of green and yellow sunflowers.
Mattie had never seen sunflowers, and was
very curious about them. He wanted to ask
Grandpa how tall they were, because he
thought they were taller than he was, and
maybe taller than Grandpa as well. But he
was afraid Grandpa might be upset if he
mentioned heights. Besides, the bridge was
quite close, and soon he'd be able to see
how tall the sunflowers were. When he
thought of them he didn't call them

sunflowers, because he didn't know the word.

Although the bridge was close, and Mattie and Grandpa kept on walking towards it, they didn't reach it.

'Grandpa, the bridge keeps being far away,' said Mattie.

'So it does,' said Grandpa.

'Why?'

'Maybe because we want it too much.'

'What d'you mean?'

'Well,' said Grandpa, 'you never get what you want too much.'

'But you do in the end, don't you?'

'Yes, but you can't tell when.'

Mattie looked at the bridge, and out of the corner of his eye, on the other side of the river, he saw the white horse. He was beyond the field of sunflowers. Only his head could be seen, high against the sky, and his tail.

But Brigand it was.

'What shall we do, then?' asked Mattie.

The bridge now seemed even further, and yet they went on walking.

'Grandpa, shall we run?' said Mattie.

'I don't think that would work, Mattie. Let's try and forget the bridge.'

'Well, what'll we do? I want it. Brigand's over there, and so is that field of big flowers.'

'The sunflowers?'

'Is that what they're called, sunflowers?'

'Yes.'

'Come on, Grandpa, let's run!' cried Mattie, clutching the cob and the apple tightly so as not to lose them while he ran.

They started running, and Mattie overtook Grandpa. But the bridge came no nearer. In fact, it seemed even further away.

'Phew,' panted Mattie, and pulled up. He sat down on the grassy bank, out of breath. Grandpa, who had been running behind him, came along slowly. He was now Mattie's height.

'You see? Running doesn't work,' he said.

'You're right, it doesn't,' said Mattie.

'Let's try not wanting it.'

'Right,' said Mattie.

They stood still, and tried not to want the bridge. Mattie half managed to, and half didn't. When he managed it, he felt the bridge was nearer. Then he would look at Brigand, and at the sunflowers, and again want to cross the bridge; and then it moved away.

'We can't manage it, Grandpa,' he said. 'How's it with you?'

'Not bad,' said Grandpa. 'I'm thinking of other things and managing not to want it too much. We'll reach it, you'll see.'

They started walking again, not in order to reach the bridge but just to have something to do.

'The market was nice, wasn't it?' Mattie said, cunningly.

They talked about things they'd seen, and things they'd done. At times the bridge came closer, at other times it stayed far away.

Then they were silent. Mattie thought of how he was going for a walk along the river, and how he didn't care a thing about the bridge, or the white horse, or the sunflowers.

But the bridge didn't believe him, and stayed far away.

Ahead of them, on the left bank, there were no horses and no sunflowers. But there was a field of newly mown hay, with heaps of fresh grass scattered about in small hillocks. The wind carried the scent of cut grass to him and Mattie breathed it in, thinking what fun it would be to dash over and take a great leap on to those piles of hay. And then jump down off the heap, and run across to another.

'Wow!' he thought, looking at the hayfield. 'It's still so far!'

'Shall we go, Grandpa?' he said, turning round.

'Where?' answered Grandpa, who was standing at the bridge, with his hand on the rail.

'The bridge!' Mattie shouted, forgetting the hayfield, and rushing up the paved slope.

'Gently, gently,' said Grandpa. 'It's not going to run away now.'

_12_

The sunflower field was huge, and the
flowers were much taller than Mattie or
Grandpa. It was a wood of flowers.

'Brigand's over there,' Mattie said
thoughtfully.

'Yes,' said Grandpa. 'We must cross over.'

The sunflowers were very beautiful, but
they were so close together that after a few

steps Mattie and Grandpa lost sight of each other.

'We can't go across like this,' said Grandpa. 'We'll lose each other.'

'But what can we do?' said Mattie.

'Let's try holding hands.'

But holding hands they couldn't get through the sunflowers.

Grandpa took off his jacket, and then his red woollen jersey. Then he put the jacket on again.

'Hot, Grandpa?' asked Mattie.

'A bit. And the jersey's going to get us through the sunflowers.'

Without another word, Grandpa pulled a thread of wool from the edge of the jersey and started to unravel it.

He gave Mattie the jersey, while he wound the red wool into a ball. Now and then the wool was broken, and Grandpa knotted the ends together. As it twisted round in his hands the red wool grew into a red ball. When the jersey's sleeves had been unravelled, the ball was bigger than Mattie's apple.

'Now we can go,' said Grandpa. 'I'll go first. You hold the wool. When I've got across, I'll shout, and you can follow the wool, winding it up.'

Carrying the ball of wool, Grandpa vanished into the sunflowers, while Mattie waited, holding the end of the wool. Time went by, and Mattie waited, holding the wool tightly and looking up at the sky. He saw ducks go by, and clouds, an aeroplane, swallows, butterflies, bumble-bees. Then he heard a shout in the distance: it was Grandpa. Mattie went into the wood of sunflowers, and started winding in the red wool, which hung quite clearly among the green stalks and leaves. The ball of wool grew bigger and bigger in his hands, and the sunflower leaves swished, partly because of the wind, and partly because Mattie was walking through them. Now and then the wool changed direction, and Mattie followed it without any trouble, winding the wool in slowly. When the ball of wool was bigger than the apple, he came out from the sunflowers and saw Grandpa sitting on the grass, waiting, and holding the end of the wool.

'Everything OK?' Grandpa asked.

'Everything OK,' said Mattie.

He looked around for Brigand.

'There he is, Grandpa!'

The horse was grazing a couple of hundred metres away, his tail flicking his flanks.

<u>13</u>

They went slowly over to him, walking
across the grass. The horse was grazing
quietly, without raising his head. But as
Mattie and Grandpa crept up he kept an
eye on them, and when they were about
fifty metres away, he perked up his ears and
neck and looked at them.

'Good boy, Brigand,' said Mattie.

But very slowly the horse moved away.

'Gosh, Grandpa, he's going away!'

'Got to be patient, Mattie. Let's try
again.'

'Shall we get him if we don't want him,
Grandpa?'

'No, because he's alive. He's got to want
something from us.'

They walked slowly towards him.
Suddenly the horse turned, and then he
looked black.

'Look, Grandpa! He's white on one side,

and black on the other!'

'So I see,' said Grandpa.

'Then he was the black horse we saw before!'

'Yes, he must have been. D'you still like him, black or white?'

Mattie considered this, then said:

'Yes, I do. It's like having two horses.'

'Then let's go up to him.'

But when they drew close to him, the horse cantered away, turning this way and that, sometimes black and sometimes white.

'What shall we do, Grandpa?' asked Mattie.

'We'll catch him,' said Grandpa.

Mattie looked at him. Grandpa was smaller than ever: he was Mattie's height now, or just a little taller.

'Grandpa . . .'

'What, Mattie?'

'Nothing. How are we going to catch Brigand?'

'Give me the apple.'

Mattie handed it to him, and Grandpa tied the apple's stalk to the end of the ball of wool, then gave Mattie the apple and unrolled half the wool, leaving it on the ground in a loose heap.

'Now throw the apple,' he said.

'At Brigand?'

'Yes, but not right up to him. That would scare him. Throw it about ten metres ahead of him. But first, give it a bite.'

'I'm not hungry, Grandpa.'

'It's for the smell. If the skin's been broken, the horse will smell it better.'

Mattie bit off a piece of apple: it was very sweet.

'Like a bit, Grandpa?' he said.

'No, thanks.'

'Then can I have your bite?'

'Of course you can. But not too big, mind, or we shan't catch Brigand.'

Mattie took a second bite, smaller this

time, and flung the apple into the grass
ahead of the horse, which, just then, was
white.

The apple flew across, with the red wool
curving against the sky behind it.

14

The apple fell in the field, and bounced.
Slowly, the wool settled in the grass and
disappeared. Almost at once the horse raised
his head and poked it towards the apple,
which was about seven or eight metres away.

'What are we to do, Grandpa?' asked
Mattie. 'If he starts eating the apple and we
pull at it, the wool will break.'

'He mustn't eat it,' said Grandpa. 'Pull it a little towards us, but not too much.'

Very, very gently Mattie pulled the wool. Unseen in the grass, it straightened, and the apple moved a few metres. The horse lowered his head and went back to munching the grass.

'He doesn't want it!' Mattie said, disappointed.

'Wait and see,' said Grandpa. 'Keep the apple where it is.'

Still eating, the horse was going ahead, taking small steps. He seemed to be moving without any special reason, but in fact was approaching the apple.

'Now pull, very gently,' said Grandpa.

'I get it!' Mattie whispered. Slowly, without a pause, he wound the wool round the ball. Without lifting his head, the horse changed tack, and moved towards the apple in the grass.

'He's coming!' murmured Mattie.

The horse was now about twenty metres

off, and seemed to be taking no notice of them.

'Shall I go on, Grandpa?'

'Yes, but very slowly. He mustn't see it, he must just smell it.'

'Why mustn't he see it?'

'Because if he sees an apple that's moving, he'll be scared and run away. But the smell doesn't frighten him. He knows a smell just comes through the air.'

'I see, Grandpa.'

Mattie went on pulling slowly. Then suddenly, he felt the wool tighten.

'Hey, Grandpa: it's stuck!'

The horse kept coming ahead, closer and closer to the apple.

'What'll I do, Grandpa? Leave it to him?'

'No. Move a couple of steps to the right, and pull again.'

Mattie moved and pulled gently. The apple started to move again. It was now about ten metres away from them.

The horse stopped, and shook his black

and white head.

'He'll run away!' whispered Mattie.

'Let's see,' said Grandpa.

The horse stood still and looked at Mattie.

'What'll I do, Grandpa? Pull?'

'Very, very gently.'

The apple could now be seen in the grass, a few steps away. Five steps, four, three.

'Now go two steps forward, slowly, and pick it up.'

Mattie went forward two steps, his heart thumping, leant down and picked up the apple.

'Shall I eat it?' he asked.

'No, break off the wool, and hold it in your hand.'

'What now, Grandpa?' said Mattie, after doing what Grandpa had told him. The horse stood quite still, watching him.

'Blow hard on the apple, in Brigand's direction,' said Grandpa.

Mattie held up the apple and blew on it.

The horse raised his head, as if asking a question.

'Now hold out the apple to him, as you would to a person,' said Grandpa.

Shaking, Mattie held out his arm.

The horse came forward very slowly, swishing his tail.

'Suppose he eats my hand, Grandpa?' said Mattie.

'Hold the apple on the palm of your hand, and don't be scared.'

Mattie put the apple on the trembling palm of his hand, afraid it would fall off.

The horse came closer. Within a yard or so of Mattie, he stretched out his neck, sniffed the apple, and put it carefully in his mouth.

'Stroke him, between his eyes and nose,' said Grandpa.

Mattie put out his hand and laid it on the horse's hard skin, half white and half black.

'There, he's caught,' said Grandpa, laughing softly.

15

Brigand was walking quietly, with Grandpa and Mattie on his back, along a white road lined with trees that had birds singing in them.

Mattie was very happy. Grandpa, sitting behind him, was a little smaller. Smaller than Mattie now, perhaps.

'Is Brigand ours, Grandpa?' asked Mattie.

'Not entirely.'

'You mean he's someone else's as well?'

'No. I mean a thing can't be owned entirely.'

'Not even a ball? Not even a stone, Grandpa?'

'Not even a ball or a stone. They're owned only a little bit.'

'But who does the part that isn't ours belong to?'

'To the world.'

Mattie was silent, considering this.

'I want the white part of the horse,' he said after a while. 'D'you think the world will want the black part?'

Grandpa laughed, and said nothing.

'No, I don't want the white part,' said Mattie. 'I want the black.'

Still Grandpa said nothing.

Then Mattie said: 'No, I don't want the white part or the black part. Or the head, or the tail.'

'Well, then?' said Grandpa.

'I'd like the whole of him. But I can't have it, can I?'

Grandpa said nothing.

'Then I'll just be with Brigand for a bit, and enjoy the ride,' said Mattie, stroking the horse's half-white and half-black mane.

Grandpa laughed again, and put his arms, which were now very small, round Mattie to give him a hug.

16

When their bottoms began to ache, Mattie and Grandpa decided to dismount. For a while they walked along beside Brigand, then they agreed to let him go. They were now close to the sea, where a thick wood of fir-trees stretched ahead, full of noisy cicadas.

'So long, Brigand!' cried Mattie, and the horse cantered off, raising dust.

They could smell the sea, and the scent of fir-trees; it was very peaceful.

'Are you hungry?' asked Grandpa.

'No, it's odd,' said Mattie. 'I'm never hungry.'

Grandpa was now quite a bit smaller than he was.

'Why are you looking at me like that, Mattie? Because I'm small?'

'Yes, Grandpa. I'm afraid you'll become so small you won't be there any more.'

'We'll see,' said Grandpa, smiling. 'When I'm very small, maybe I'll start growing again, and become a giant-Grandpa.'

Mattie looked at him, and said nothing.

'Shall we play a game?' Grandpa said.

'Yes, let's! What game is it?'

'Treasure hunting.'

'How do we play that?'

'We follow the treasure map.'

'And where's that?'

'On our hand.'

'Which hand? We've got four between us – two of mine and two of yours!'

They looked at their four hands. There were interesting lines on all of them.

'It's hard to tell, Grandpa.'

'Maybe there's just a single map.'

'How's that, Grandpa?'

Grandpa put his hands together, palms upwards, and said:

'Put yours together.'

Mattie put his hands close to Grandpa's, until their fingers were touching.

'Closer, Mattie,' said Grandpa.

They linked fingers, Grandpa's thin and white, Mattie's plump and pink. Their palms were now close, making a big map.

'Where's the treasure, Grandpa?'

'We need a sign,' said Grandpa. 'Let's wait.'

They sat there under the fir-trees in that odd position, like a couple of friendly beggars waiting for alms.

The wind was warm and sweet-smelling, and it lifted their hair – Mattie's black and Grandpa's white. Grandpa's hands were warm and dry, and smaller than Mattie's.

Mattie looked at the lines on his hands. 'Will there be a sign, Grandpa?' he asked.

'Sure to be,' said Grandpa.

17

There was a fir-tree near them, and as they waited Mattie saw something odd on its bark. It looked like a grasshopper, but it was quite still and transparent.

'Grandpa, what's that?'

'That thing on the tree trunk?'

'Yes.'

'It's a kind of shell. It's the skin of a grasshopper. Some insects, when they grow, form a new one inside the old one, because their outer casing doesn't grow with them. The insect grows bigger, and breaks out of the old skin, which is called a shell.'

'How odd,' said Mattie. 'It reminds me of an insect. Can I take it, afterwards?'

'Yes.'

They sat in silence, waiting for a sign. Some needles fell on the map from the fir-tree, but flew away at once. Then, noiselessly, a tiny fly landed on Mattie's left hand.

'Is that the sign, Grandpa?'

'Yes, let's have a look.'

They saw where the fly had landed, and where they should find the treasure, just where two lines met on the palm of Mattie's hand.

'Had a good look?' asked Grandpa.

'I think so. And anyway, if I forget, I'll still have the fly tickling me.'

The fly flew off.

'But where are we now, the two of us?' said Mattie. 'I mean, on the map.'

'We must look and see,' said Grandpa, and looked around him.

He nodded towards the left.

'That path may be the thin line on my right hand,' he said. 'So, we're where I've got that little black mole on my skin. Can you see it?'

'Yes, but are we sure, Grandpa? It might be the thin line on my left hand, there, near the treasure.'

'Let's have a think,' said Grandpa.

74

After a while Mattie said:

'The path looks like my line, and it also looks like yours. So what are we to do?'

'We can try both,' said Grandpa.

'How? Are there two treasures?'

'I don't think so. But first, let's take it that the path's the line on your hand. If it is, then the treasure's near by.'

They took the map apart and got up, counted their footsteps, and found the place that corresponded to the place where the fly had landed. A dry bush was growing there.

'Shall we dig, Grandpa?'

'Yes, let's.'

At first the earth was hard, but as they dug it gradually became soft and dark. Mattie found a piece of round, curved glass, like the lens in a pair of spectacles.

'Is this the treasure, Grandpa?'

'I don't think so.'

'I want to keep it, though. I like it.'

They dug deeper, but found no treasure underground.

'So the way to go must be different,' said Grandpa. 'The path must be the line on my hand. There aren't any others.'

They went back to where they had started, and made the map out of their hands again. Then they walked along what seemed to be the new path. But after taking a few steps, Mattie stopped.

'The shell!' he said, and ran back to prise the grasshopper's stiff casing off the tree trunk. Then he went back to Grandpa.

'If I put it in my pocket, it'll be spoilt,' he said.

'Wait a minute,' said Grandpa. He took a tobacco tin out of his pocket and emptied it on the ground. By now he was a lot smaller than Mattie, and had to look up when he spoke to him.

A little tobacco blew into Mattie's nose, and he sneezed and laughed.

'Why are you throwing your tobacco away, Grandpa?' he asked, his eyes smarting and full of tears.

'Because I don't want it any more,' said Grandpa.

They put the shell in the tin, which was big enough to hold it. Then they started walking again, along the straight path.

18

The map was right: every crossing or curve in the lines of their hands corresponded to a crossing or a curve in the path. But they had to be careful, especially when they were on the land shown on Grandpa's hand, because it was full of small paths and dried-up streams, short slopes and turnings. Then, when they reached the part that corresponded to the map on Mattie's hands, they walked more quickly. The fir-trees grew thickly here, and they were close to the sea.

Through the sweet-smelling tree trunks they could see the blue water, and they heard the constant murmur of the waves.

Grandpa was now tiny, walking fast and firmly ahead of Mattie, who was watching him. Maybe, Mattie thought, the treasure was a medicine to make him bigger.

When they reached the place where the fly had landed, they stopped to rest.

'It's under here, isn't it?' said Mattie.

'If the map's right, it should be,' answered Grandpa.

'But who put the treasure there?' said Mattie.

'Who knows? Brigands, or pirates.'

'But won't they come back to get it?'

'Maybe they've forgotten it, or been drowned. Or maybe they will come back.'

'And they won't find it,' laughed Mattie.

For half an hour they dug away cheerfully, cooled by the sea breeze. Mattie was afraid that Grandpa would fall in the hole, and kept an eye on him.

Then they struck something hard; they dug out more earth and stones, and saw a trunk made of wood, iron and green velvet.

'This is it!' cried Mattie, helping Grandpa to open it. But inside there were only some roots from the fir-trees, which had got into the trunk through holes in the side of it.

'What a shame!' said Mattie, sitting on the edge of the hole. But he wasn't too disappointed: the fun lay in the search.

'The pirates came back, didn't they?' he asked.

'Looks like it,' said Grandpa, climbing out of the hole. 'But they left this.'

And he showed Mattie a gold coin, with the face of a king of Spain from long ago on it.

'Better than nothing, Grandpa!' said Mattie, and made the coin glint in the sun.

'Are you hungry now?' asked Grandpa, lying down on his back. He was now no longer than the trunk they had found.

'No, I'm not,' said Mattie. 'But I may be soon.'

They looked up at the sky through the branches of the fir-trees, breathing in the scent of resin and of the sea. The cicadas were singing loudly, and it was hot. And there was a strange murmur, a very slight clicking sound.

Maybe they slept for a while.

'You asleep, Grandpa?' said Mattie.

'No, I'm looking at the sky.'

'It's nice, isn't it? Blue and gold.'

'How d'you mean, blue and gold?'

'Blue sky, gold branches,' said Mattie, and yawned.

'So that's where the gold went,' said Grandpa merrily.

'Where?'

'Into the fir-tree,' said Grandpa. 'The roots took it, and made the tree gold. It's the first living gold I've ever seen.'

They lay there, looking at the wonderful tree, listening to the clicking murmur of the branches, and admiring the endless, dazzling golden needles.

Maybe they slept again.

19

When they awoke, Mattie wanted to go for
a swim. He ran on to the beach, undressed
and ran into the sea, splashing and shouting
in the shallow water. Grandpa, who was
now tiny, stayed sitting on the beach
watching Mattie's fun.

Suddenly, in the distance, they saw a
sailing ship.

'A pirate ship!' shouted Mattie, running

up on to the beach.

'Looks like it,' said Grandpa, shading his eyes with his hand to get a better look.

Bobbing on the green waves, the ship was slowly coming ashore.

'They're coming here, Grandpa!'

'So they are.'

Though the ship looked far away, it was actually quite close, because it was a small vessel, just about eight metres long, and full of small pirates. But they weren't children: they were real pirates, with beards and whiskers, but dwarfs.

Grandpa and Mattie looked at them curiously, and Mattie put on his clothes.

'What'll we do, Grandpa? Run away?'

'D'you want to?' asked Grandpa.

'I'd like to see them close up.'

'Let's wait, then.'

They waited until the ship stopped about fifty metres from the beach. They saw the pirates run to the ship's side, shouting, and lower three boats.

'Shall we run away now?' asked Mattie.

'D'you want to?'

'Well, I'd like to talk to them. They may be friendly pirates.'

'Maybe. But suppose they're the ones who buried the treasure?'

The three boats, full of small pirates, were now near the beach.

'Let's be off, then!' said Mattie, and set off, running towards the wood. He heard a cry behind him, and turned. Grandpa, being so small, was having trouble with the sand. Mattie went back, picked him up and started running again; but he found it difficult, and kept tripping. The pirates ran as smoothly as cats, though, and were catching up.

'They've won, Mattie,' said Grandpa. 'Put me down, and let's wait for them.'

'Gotcher!' shouted a pirate, seizing Mattie's elbow.

'D'you give in, or fight?' said another.

'Give in, of course,' said Grandpa. 'You're too many for us.'

20

Mattie and Grandpa were taken to a square tower which stood on the beach not far away. The pirate chief searched them, and found the tobacco tin with the shell, the round piece of glass and the gold coin in it.

He gave everything back except the coin. 'Where did you find this?' he said. 'This must be part of a treasure.'

Grandpa, who was now smaller than the pirates, looked up at Mattie.

'I've always had it,' he said. 'It was left to me by my grandfather.'

'That would be my great-great grandpa,' said Mattie.

The pirate chief looked at them.

'Tough guys, eh?' he said. 'We'll leave you without food, while we rest. That'll make you tell us where the treasure is!'

He shut them in a cell which looked out on to the sea through an iron grating. It had a wooden door, with a small window half-way up it.

Three pirates were on guard outside the door. By standing on tiptoe, Mattie could just see them through the window.

'Why did you say the coin was left to you, Grandpa?' he said softly. 'In any case, even if they go to the place, they won't find a thing.'

'But if they find the tree, and notice that it has golden needles, they'll want to cut it down,' said Grandpa.

'Then you were right to tell a fib,
Grandpa,' said Mattie.

'Hungry?'

'A bit. Not very.'

'See if there's anyone out there,' said
Grandpa.

Mattie looked, but saw that the pirates
were some distance away.

'No one, Grandpa.'

Grandpa then took the corn cob from his
trousers and said:

'Well hidden, wasn't it? If we're hungry,
we'll eat it!'

'And then?'

'Then we'll see.'

They looked at the sea through the
window: Mattie held Grandpa up, because
he was so small.

'Try shaking the bars, Mattie,' said
Grandpa. 'I'm not strong enough.'

Mattie took hold of the bars, and pushed
and pulled.

'It's solid, Grandpa. Maybe if I pulled terribly hard I'd manage it. No, I can't.'

'Well, we'll have another think later. Now I'll tell you a story, if you like.'

Mattie loved Grandpa's stories. At home, he told him one every day. They were sometimes the same story, and sometimes new ones.

'Would you like an old one or a new one?' said Grandpa.

Mattie sat down and picked Grandpa up.

'A new one, please.'

And Grandpa told him a new story, about the devil's three saucepans.

21

When the story was over, the pirate chief peered in.

'Are you going to tell us where the treasure is?' he said.

'I've always had that coin,' said Grandpa.

'You'll die of hunger!' cried the pirate chief, and ran off.

Mattie was feeling really hungry now.

They picked up the corn cob, but the grains were too hard.

'Pick them all off, one by one, and take them over to the window,' said Grandpa.

Mattie did what Grandpa told him to do, while Grandpa set the lens at a special angle, leaning it against a piece of wood. A ray of sunshine went through the glass, and made a patch of very bright light on the windowsill.

'Put a grain there,' said Grandpa.

Mattie put one down and waited. After a

while, pop! – the grain swelled up and burst.
Mattie picked it up and ate it: it was soft
and tasty.

One by one, the grains were cooked by
the sun, and he was no longer hungry.

Evening came. The pirates were singing
in the tower's big room, and drinking
scented wine in small metal cups. Then they
fell down drunk on the floor, except for two
or three, who stayed on guard outside the
cell door.

Mattie looked out and said:

'What are your names?'

'Deathshead,' said one.

'Crossbones,' said another.

'Parrotface,' said the third.

'Is it fun being a pirate?' Mattie asked.

'Well, it's certainly not boring,' said Deathshead.

'Aren't you ever seasick?' said Mattie.

'If you were, you'd never become a pirate,' said Parrotface.

Mattie would have liked to ask more questions, but he felt sleepy, and lay down on the wooden bench in the cell. Grandpa was asleep too and snoring a little. But the pirates, who were full of red wine, were snoring more loudly outside.

22

Early in the morning, no cock crowed to
wake them, because there were no cocks
near by. It was Grandpa who woke Mattie,
saying quietly:

'Wake up, Mattie. We're going to
escape.'

Mattie sat up at once.

'But how are we going to do it, Grandpa?
The door's shut, and we can't get through
the window!'

'Wait,' said Grandpa, and went over to
the door.

'Hey, psst!' he said, and at once the faces
of Deathshead, Crossbones and Parrotface
appeared.

'What is it?' they said, looking down at
tiny Grandpa.

'If we have a competition, and you win,
then I'll tell you where the treasure is,' said
Grandpa.

The three pirates looked at one another.

'What sort of competition?' they said softly, so as not to wake the others.

'Mind you, we're not opening this door!'

'Is it a card game?'

'No,' said Grandpa. 'It's a tug of war.'

'What sort?'

'Well, the two of us in here against the three of you out there,' said Grandpa. 'You put a strong rope through the little window in the door, and hold your end. You pull from there, we pull from in here, and whoever manages to pull the others a couple of steps along wins.'

'And suppose we win, then you'll tell us where the treasure is?'

'Certainly,' said Grandpa.

'And what if we lose?' said Parrotface. 'You don't expect us to open the door, do you?'

'No, we'll be playing just because we're bored,' said Grandpa.

The three pirates talked it over among

themselves, whispering and glancing at the others, who were fast asleep.

'Right,' they said, and went to find a rope, which they handed in through the window in the door.

'Ready?' they said.

Grandpa winked at Mattie and said quietly:

'Tie our end to the bars on the window – hurry!'

And to the pirates outside he called:

'Just a minute, please!'

Mattie quickly tied the rope to the window bars, and came back to Grandpa.

'Now what?' he whispered.

'We'll be pulling too, but in the right direction.'

'You ready?' the pirates called impatiently from outside.

'Ready!' cried Grandpa, seizing the cord with Mattie.

'Ready, steady, go!' cried the pirates outside the door, and began tugging with all their might. Mattie and Grandpa, although he was so small, were pulling in the same direction. The grating in the window came away in a cloud of dust and fell on to the floor.

Grandpa and Mattie leapt through the window on to the beach and ran and ran as fast as their legs could carry them.

23

Grandpa was now so small that he got left behind, so Mattie picked him up and ran off along the beach. Now and then he turned round to see if the pirates were getting close. But he and Grandpa were safe.

Mattie ran and ran, clambering over rocks and racing across sands, until he reached a beautiful inlet of golden sand. There he stopped to rest, holding Grandpa in his arms like a baby.

'We made it, didn't we, Grandpa?' he said.

'Easily,' said Grandpa.

They looked at the sea, which was as smooth as a silver ribbon.

'Are you going to vanish, Grandpa?' Mattie asked.

'No, wait and see,' said Grandpa, and looked out to sea again. Then he said:

'Let's go home now. Which way would you like to go?'

'How many ways are there?' said Mattie.

He got up, and walked through the fir-trees, over a bridge, along a road. He was holding Grandpa in his hands, because he was too small to walk through the wood or along the ground. He held him sitting in one hand, with the other in front of him to stop him falling.

'Grandpa?' he said.

'Yes, Mattie?'

'As you're so little, why is your voice like it was before?'

'What d'you mean?'

'Shouldn't your voice be little too?'

'It is a bit,' said Grandpa. 'But you can hear me because you've got good ears.'

'Look, over there – that's the sunflower field!' Mattie cried. 'Grandpa, we're back at the sunflowers!'

'Maybe it's the same one, or maybe it's another one. D'you want to go across it?'

'Yes.'

Mattie walked slowly, carrying Grandpa,

and picking the right path. Ahead, he could
hear the sound of the river, and that was
where he was going, among the big round
sweet-smelling flowers.

The sound of the river came closer and
closer.

'Here we are!' cried Mattie, coming out
on to the path beside the river. 'And look,
there's the bridge, too!'

'Want to stop and rest a bit, Mattie?' said Grandpa, when they were at the highest point on the bridge.

'Yes,' said Mattie. 'And look at the sun.'

24

Mattie sat down on the side of the bridge and looked at the red sun in the sky ahead. It was sunset.

'Lift me up a bit, please,' said Grandpa. 'I can't see very well from here.'

'Like to stand on my head, Grandpa?' said Mattie.

'Good idea! It'll be like being in a field,' said Grandpa.

Mattie put him carefully up on to his hair. Grandpa was now very tiny.

They stayed there, looking at the sunset.

'It's pretty, isn't it?' said Mattie.

'It is,' said Grandpa.

The river made a wide curve ahead of them, and the water was as red as the sky. Red and yellow and orange.

'I wonder where Brigand is,' Mattie said. But he didn't hear Grandpa's answer, because he had already fallen sleep. He slept for a few minutes, or maybe for an hour. A cool breeze woke him, and he saw that the sky had turned from dark red to blue, with a few very bright stars.

He could no longer feel Grandpa in his hair, and his heart began to beat hard.

'Grandpa!' he called.

'Yes, Mattie?'

'Oh, you're there!'

'Of course I am. You've slept a bit, haven't you?'

'Yes.'

'Did you dream?'

'I think so, but I can't remember what.'

'Look at the stars, Mattie. D'you know them?'

Mattie looked up.

'That's the Plough, isn't it?' he said, pointing. 'You told me that when I was small.'

'Yes, I remember.'

Mattie was silent, wondering how Grandpa had become now. He couldn't feel the smallest weight on his head.

'We must go now,' Grandpa said.

Mattie put up a hand to take him, but couldn't find him.

'Where are you?' he said.

'I'm here. Look gently.'

Very gently Mattie patted his hair. Grandpa was as small as a chocolate drop. He picked him up carefully and looked at him in the dim evening light. He could

hardly see him, and he felt like a tickle in the palm of his hand, the way the fly had felt in the wood earlier on.

'What shall we do, Grandpa?' said Mattie. 'I'm afraid of losing you, you're so little. Shall I put you in my pocket?'

'Better not, Mattie.'

'So what, then?'

'Let's wait a bit,' said Grandpa. 'For the moment, close your fist and hold me there, and we'll go home. We'll find a way, you'll see.'

Very, very gently Mattie clenched his fist, and walked across the bridge. He now knew the way.

They went through the town where the market had been held. There was no one about, and the streets were quiet and dark.

Mattie spoke now and then, so as to hear Grandpa's voice.

'There's no market now, Grandpa.'

'Yes, it's late.'

A little further on Mattie said:

'There are street lamps along the river, Grandpa.'

'Good, that'll make it easier to walk, Mattie.'

And further on still:

'We've got to the canal now, Grandpa.'

'Where there's the little bridge?'

'Yes.'

'Then we're nearly there.'

Mattie walked on, but he could feel nothing in his hand now.

'Grandpa?' he said.

'Yes, Mattie?'

'Nothing: I just wanted to hear you.'

'Here I am,' said Grandpa. 'Smelling of pepper!'

Mattie pulled up suddenly, right under a street lamp.

'What was that? Smelling of pepper?'

'That's right,' said Grandpa, from his fist.

Mattie put his hand up to his face and opened it very very slowly; and he could see nothing.

'Grandpa,' he said softly.

'Here I am,' said Grandpa, who was quite invisible.

'I can't see you, Grandpa.'

'That's because I've become even smaller. I'm here.'

'But what were you saying about pepper?'

'Can't you smell it?'

'No.'

'Are you sure? Have a good sniff, Mattie!'

Mattie raised the palm of his hand up to his nose.

'I don't smell it, Grandpa.'

'Harder,' said Grandpa. 'You must sniff harder, like I used to with tobacco, d'you remember?'

Then Mattie sniffed as hard as he could, and the air whistled through his nostrils.

'I can't smell pepper at all, Grandpa,' he said.

'Well, there wasn't any,' said Grandpa.

But his voice no longer came from Mattie's hand: it seemed to come from around and inside Mattie.

'What's happened, Grandpa?' he asked.

'I played a little trick on you, Mattie. I made you sniff your hand hard, so as to get inside you. If I'd asked you to put me in your mouth, I don't think you'd have done it. Or you'd have hated doing it.'

'So you're inside me now?'

'Yes.'

'And that's your voice?'

'Yes, but now only you can hear it.'

'And how are you, Grandpa?'

'Fine, Mattie. A boy's a good place to live in.'

Mattie was quiet for a moment, thinking.

'Now we'll go home, shall we?' he said.

'Yes, it's time to,' said Grandpa.

25

Under a lamp-post, a few steps ahead, hanging in the air, on the river bank, was a door which Mattie recognized.

He went up to it, opened it, and went in.

In Grandpa's bedroom, everything was just as it had been when he left: Mum, Dad, the uncles, six grandchildren and a few family friends. Some of them were crying, others had been crying.

On the bed lay Grandpa, pale and still.

Mattie walked past the people and went back to Mum, just where he'd been beside her before the walk. He looked up to see if the fly was there, but didn't see it.

He looked at Grandpa on the bed and saw that he was very still and very pale.

'Grandpa,' he said in a very low voice.

'Yes?' said Grandpa.

'Where are you?'

'I'm here.'

'Here, not there — right?'

'Right,' said Grandpa. 'Over there, that's just the shell.'

'That's what I thought,' said Mattie, and smiled a little.

He heard a deep sigh, looked at Mum, who seemed so sad, and took her hand. She looked at him and pressed his hand.

That day, and the next, everyone was very sad.

Out of respect for their silence, Mattie never laughed, even when Grandpa said funny things to him, as he did sometimes.

When they had taken the shell to the graveyard, Dad said to Mattie:

'You loved Grandpa a lot, didn't you?'

'Of course I love him,' said Mattie.

For a moment Dad was puzzled, and looked at him without speaking.

'Well, he's no longer here,' Dad said after a bit. 'But . . .'

Mattie looked at him expectantly. It

seemed as though Dad had something to say but didn't know how to say it.

'D'you mean he's still here?' said Mattie.

Dad bit his lip.

'Yes, that's it,' he said. 'Someone we love stays with us for the whole of our life. D'you understand?'

Mattie smiled, and tweaked his father's beard a little, as he often did, for fun.